Tales of
Belva Jean
Copenhagen

Books by Sandra Dutton

The Magic of Myrna C. Waxweather
The Cinnamon Hen's Autumn Day
Tales of Belva Jean Copenhagen

Tales of
Belva Jean
Copenhagen

written and illustrated by
Sandra Dutton

ATHENEUM   1989   NEW YORK

For my mother and father

Atheneum
Macmillan Publishing Company
866 Third Avenue, New York, NY 10022
Collier Macmillan Canada, Inc.
First Edition
Printed in the United States of America

10 9 8 7 6 5 4 3 2 1

Library of Congress Cataloging-in-Publication Data
Dutton, Sandra.
Tales of Belva Jean Copenhagen / written and illustrated
by Sandra Dutton — 1st ed. p. cm.
Summary: Sixth-grader Belva Jean shares stories of her classmates,
her neighbors, and her family.
ISBN 0–689–31463–9
[1. Family life — Fiction. 2. Schools — Fiction.] I. Title.
PZ7. D952Tal 1989
[Fic] — dc19
88 — 27492 CIP AC

Contents

Preface / 1

The Sleeping Beauty Bridal Gown / 3

The Most Normal Mother / 12

What Granny Kept in Her Grips / 21

The Fourth of July Party / 31

Me and Buster / 40

Uncle Abraham's Cabin / 47

Standard English / 58

Afterword / 74

Preface

I thought I would put one of these onto my book because I seen one in a couple of other books of stories. It's where the author tells the reader what to look out for and where she got the ideas for what she's written up.

Well, I ain't going to tell you what to look for, except a lot of true stories about my friends and family. My daddy, he works down at the Palmer Thermometer Company putting mercury into thermometers, and Mama, she makes patchwork quilts and takes care of my baby brother, Buster. My best friends are JaneEllen Hazard and Faron Lavella. You'll meet them, too.

Now you might say, "*Tales of Belva Jean Copenhagen* — that sounds like a lot of made-up stuff," but it ain't. It's pure true-life adventure. Everything I tell you in these stories happened — even the part about catching the Frisbee at the Fourth of July party and wearing a necktie skirt to school.

I will tell you, though, that I first called this book *Belva Jean Goes to Africa*. It was all about me and Faron tracking poachers. Problem was, I didn't know what the poachers looked like or what they was poaching for. 'Course I could have made it all up (I'm good at that), but people that write a lot say your first book ought to be something you know.

So there you got it. This here is what I know.

The Sleeping Beauty Bridal Gown

We was all out on the playground at my new school, Everett Akers, standing up there in the corner by the jungle gym. It was April — I'd only been there a few days — but I was thinking how much I liked this school even better than my old one. The kids was nicer, the playground was bigger, and the water in the drinking fountains was a whole lot colder.

Then Dixie Lee Combs, she come up to me in a brand-new pair of blue corduroy pants, so stiff they looked like they was still on the hanger, and she said to me, she said, "Belva Jean, how's come you wear such old, worn-out clothes?"

Well, I never considered that I wore old, worn-out clothes. Mama, she was always want-

3

ing me to wear some of them patchwork dresses she made and sold, but I never wanted to wear none of them. I just liked jeans. And I guess everybody at my old school was used to me, because they never said nothing about my clothes. So I said, "What do you mean?"

And Dixie Lee said, "Them jeans. You're always wearing them old, worn-out jeans."

Them jeans I was wearing that day — Can't Bust 'Ems — was patched at the knees with yellow duck swatches Mama pulled out of a wallpaper book. We picked them up at the Goodwill, and my high-top tennis shoes — black canvas with white stripes on the side — we picked them up from the rummage sale at St. Vincent's. I didn't want to tell Dixie Lee that, though, so I said, "Problem was, when we moved, my clothes, they was all stolen by the CIA. That's why I'm wearing these, till my new order comes in."

"Yeah?" Dixie Lee said. "Well, what did you order?"

I could tell by the way she said this she didn't believe me, so I said, "It's not what I ordered that's important to me, it's what I lost. I lost a bunch of good stuff."

4

"Like what?" Dixie Lee squeezed her hands into her front pockets.

"Well," I said — and I seen Janice Decker was coming over to listen, too — "I had me a Jeeter Cummings Rhinestone Cowgirl Shirt."

"Jeeter Cummings!" Janice Decker said. Jeeter just got inducted into the Country Hall of Fame. "You wear it much?"

"Every holiday I wore it," I said. "And sometimes, at my old school, they asked me to sing."

"You a singer?" Janice said this like she was halfway interested.

"Well, I *was*," I said. I sung "Two-Time Lover" and "Nine to Five" like Jeeter Cummings.

"Well, sing us something," Dixie Lee said.

"Nah," I said. "I don't feel like singing no more on account of losing all my clothes."

"I guess I wouldn't, neither," Dixie Lee said. "What else you lose?"

Two other girls come up to listen — Eva Jones and JaneEllen Hazard, so I knew I had to think up something good. I said, "Had me a coat of genuine rabbits' feet — the whole thing, all rabbits' feet."

"Lucky you," JaneEllen said. "Double lucky."

"Yes, I was," I said. "I was so lucky I could

put money into a Coke machine and get three cans instead of one."

"I think that was just an accident," Eva Jones said.

"Maybe," I said. "But it worked every time. Now I ain't had nothing but bad luck."

"It'll change," JaneEllen said. "Just tell us what else you lost." You could tell she didn't want to hear no hard-luck stories. Just about them outfits.

"Let me see," I said. "I had me a red velvet cape."

"Red velvet!"

"Red velvet's not all," I said. "It was lined with silver and gold threads, and in the back was a pocket full of flashlights."

"Flashlights, what for?"

"Exploring. I like to go through haunted houses."

Eva Jones looked at Dixie Lee, and Dixie Lee said, "What else you lose?"

"Well, I had me sixteen pair of high heels."

"Sixteen pair!"

"Yeah, they was all different kinds. I had me some with glass heels and some with solid gold ankle straps. And I had me one pair so high

Mama said I ought to have crutches."

"Now that's high," Janice Decker said.

"Yes, it is, and I had me one pair with a secret compartment in the heel."

"For keeping what?" Dixie Lee asked.

"Fingerprints, but I can't tell you whose because I'm a-sworn to secrecy."

"What else you lose?" Eva Jones asked.

"Had me some fingernails."

"Fingernails?"

"Yes, genuine fake fingernails, all painted with birds and flowers and things."

"Was they long?"

"Was they! They was so long I couldn't hold a pen to write my name, so teacher used to let me sit and lick envelopes."

"Now I know you're making this up," Dixie Lee said.

"Yeah, me, too," Eva Jones said.

"Don't matter," Janice Decker said.

"No, it don't matter at all," JaneEllen said.

Janice Decker and JaneEllen, they was the leaders, so I knowed it truly didn't matter. I could have said anything, long as it was good.

JaneEllen said to me, she said, "What was your most favorite outfit? Just tell us what was your most favorite, best one?"

"Oh," I said, "I had a lot of them. There was my Dogwood Festival Dancing Dress and my pure silk Parachute Jumping Skirt and my May Day Flower Princess Dress. My most favorite best one?"

"Come on, just pick one," she said.

The 12:30 bell was about to ring, so I figured she wanted one last good thing to think about before math.

"Okay," I said. "There was my Sleeping Beauty Bridal Gown. I wore it every year, first day of fall. It was all in white satin, and it come to here," and I showed them the line on my tennis shoe where it hit, "and then there was red roses around the neck and mink fur around the wrists, and diamonds all up and down the front, and then there was this train," and I showed them how it come off the shoulders in the back and went for a good thirty feet. I walked over to the fence and showed them how long it was. "And when I wore it, kids would pick up my train and follow me into school."

"You was really something," JaneEllen said.

"Yes, I was," I said.

Then the bell rung. And was I glad.

9

But two weeks later, Dixie Lee Combs run into some girl from my old school and she asked her, "Did Belva Jean Copenhagen wear a lot of fancy clothes?"

And this girl, I never did find out who she was, she said no, she just wore jeans.

So Dixie Lee Combs, she said to me, right in front of everybody, "I got it from a girl at your other school that you never wore nothing except them jeans."

But by that time, Mama had made me a necktie skirt, the only kind of patchwork I like. I wore it on the last day of school. And out on the playground, when I twirled around, I looked like a giant top.

Dixie Lee Combs said, "Is that one of them new outfits you ordered?"

"Sort of," I said. "I ordered it from my mama. She made it."

Then Eva Jones said, "Well, where did she get all them neckties?"

I started to tell her how they come out of a surprise bag from Jim's Bargain City, but then I said, "This here one" — it was blue with a peacock on it — "once belonged to Prince Charles."

JaneEllen said, "Let me touch it."

And Janice Decker wanted to touch it, too.

But Dixie Lee said, "Sure, Belva Jean, and the one next to it belonged to the king of Siam."

"No, really," I said. "Mama was at this yard sale at that big house down on Sloan—" They all knew the one I meant. It's got a big tower on one corner, all painted up like a castle, with a grand piano in the living room. You can see the lid through the window. "And the lady who lives there, she come out when Mama was looking at the ties and she said this here one the prince give to her husband when they was having dinner at the palace. She said her husband had lost his luggage at the London Airport."

"Why didn't she want to keep it?" Eva Jones said.

"Because she don't like the way Prince Charles is always running off to Scotland," I said.

"I don't believe it," Eva Jones said.

"I don't, neither," Dixie Lee said.

But JaneEllen said, "I do."

And Janice Decker said, "Me, too."

That's the thing about JaneEllen and Janice. They don't mind a good story now and then.

The Most Normal Mother

Mama, when she eats cherries, likes to line the seeds up in a parade. I've told her, "You know, Mama, I wish you would wrap them seeds up in a napkin."

"Well, Belva Jean, if you don't like it, just don't look."

But that ain't the only thing she does when she eats. She takes her ice and crunches it real loud and fast, like a hamster. "Mama, why are you always chewing your ice?" I ask her.

"Because it cools off my mouth."

Then she'll take her napkin sometimes and tuck it up under her chin.

I'll say, "Mama, that's for babies."

She'll say, "Belva Jean, grown people don't

want to ruin their good clothes, neither."

Then she'll eat spinach by twirling it on her fork.

I'll say, "Mama, that's the way you do spaghetti."

And she'll say, "Belva Jean, whatever comes in strings is easiest ate if it's twirled on a fork."

"But it ain't good manners," I'll say.

"Well," she'll say, "if I'm out somewhere, I'll eat the way Emily Vanderbilt eats."

So when the school had its Mother-Daughter Banquet, you better believe I went over the rules with Mama on how I wanted her to eat.

I took the menu home, and we sat down at the kitchen table — my baby brother, Buster, was having his nap — and I read to her what they was having:

Bing Cherries in Cup
Stuffed Breast of Chicken
Fresh Garden Peas
Princess Potatoes
Fudge Brownie à la Mode
Iced Tea with Lemon

13

Then I went over the rules, trying not to sound too worried or too bossy.

"Mama, when we have our cherries, what are you going to do with them pits?"

"I don't know," Mama said. "I might just put them into my potatoes." She thought this was funny.

"Well, don't line them up," I said.

"Belva Jean, don't worry."

"And when we have chicken," I said, "don't pull the stuffing out, even if it's something funny."

"What do you mean, something funny?"

"I mean something that looks funny, like rice or nuts or raisins or little bits of vegetables."

"Belva Jean, I know that," she said. "When a person is out, she either eats her food as is or she puts a napkin over it."

But I was worried, so I thought I'd better mention one more thing. "And when we have tea, just for once, don't chew your ice. I think the principal's giving a speech, and the people at our table want to be able to hear."

"Don't worry," Mama said. "I'll just suck on the ice."

But I wanted to tell her, "Just don't mess with the ice at all."

I was worried because I figured everybody's mother would be perfect but mine. I figured JaneEllen Hazard's mother would be tall and blond, like her, and would have on a pretty blue dress. And Dixie Lee Combs's mother, I figured she would be little tiny, like Dixie, and have a nice, quiet voice. "Don't talk in a loud voice," I said.

"How would you like me to talk?" she said.

"Nice and soft." Sometimes, in a crowd, Mama's the loudest one of all.

"Are you sure you want me to go?"

"Yes, I want you to go, but you can't be loud." Then I said, "What are you going to wear?"

"Well, if bad comes to worst," she said, "I can always wear my gypsy skirt and headdress." Mama dressed up like a gypsy for Halloween. But I didn't want her wearing nothing as silly as that.

"No, really," I said. "What are you going to wear?"

"I don't know."

So we walked down the hall and went through her closet together. "How about this?" she said, and she took out a sequined evening dress she'd bought at a garage sale.

"No, this ain't that formal."

15

"Well, how about this?" And she took out some white pedal pushers.

"Oh, come on, Mama." She don't have many clothes, but she's got a few good dresses. "Let me look."

So I looked through and found a nice blue dress.

"Now, are you sure this is all right? This is what you want me to wear?"

"I'm sure," I said. "You'll look real nice. And wear your heels, too." Mama had two pair.

"Well, how do you want me to walk?" she said, and she sort of strutted across the bedroom, like she needed me to teach her how to walk. She wasn't being serious now.

"Just walk normal," I said, and I walked across the room, trying to show her what normal looked like.

The night of the banquet, Daddy and Buster took us down to the school in the truck. The banquet was in the cafeteria and the Girls' Band was having a concert first.

I went over the rules with Mama once again before we walked in. Don't chew ice, don't line up your pits, don't tuck in your napkin, don't

16

talk too loud, walk normal, and be friendly at all times.

And Mama said, "What do you mean, 'Be friendly'?"

I said, "Smile a lot and say hello." Then I added, "But not too loud."

Anyway, there was other girls arriving with their mothers, and we was all clomping in our good shoes down to the cafeteria, and I was hoping me and Mama looked as normal as they all did.

The cafeteria was decorated with red tulips and pink carnations, and there was a banner across the top that said "Everett Akers Mother-Daughter Banquet." Then, up front on the stage, the Girls' Band was tuning up.

I introduced Mama to my teacher, Mrs. Comer, and Mrs. Comer said, "Good evening. What a pleasure it is to meet you, Mrs. Copenhagen."

And Mama said, "Good evening. How nice it is to meet you, Mrs. Comer." Just as normal as Mrs. Comer.

We walked all the way across to where the sixth grade was supposed to sit, and, what do you know, JaneEllen Hazard was already there,

but if that was her mother sitting next to her, I just couldn't believe it. She was as old as my granny — in fact, I thought she was her granny — but JaneEllen introduced me and said, "I'd like you to meet my mother."

"Good evening," I said, and I introduced my mother. But I couldn't believe it. JaneEllen's mother had a mustache. Not like a man's, exactly, but it was there, all these straggly hairs across her upper lip. And she didn't look at all like JaneEllen. Just kind of heavyset with little bitty eyes and a wide neck.

Dixie Lee Combs's mother, she wasn't what I expected, neither. She was real skinny with a big gob of rouge on each cheek and a big bow in her hair that made her look like Minnie Mouse. But she had the same little bitty voice like Dixie. "Evening, Belva Jean," she said.

Janice Decker come in with her mama just behind us. She looked normal enough, in a red dress carrying a black patent leather pocketbook, but as soon as the principal asked us all to stand and sing the national anthem, Mrs. Decker sort of went all out like she was doing a solo. She warbled real loud on the high notes and lingered on them longer than the band did.

19

Mama leaned over and said to me, "Do you think she'll make the opera?"

Then when we all sat down and the Girls' Band played "Beautiful Ohio," Mrs. Hazard took out a pile of Blue Chip stamps and began pasting them into her wish book.

JaneEllen didn't say nothing. She just kept listening to the band. Then the waiters (sixth-grade boys) handed out the dinner. Right away Mrs. Hazard took cherry juice by the spoonful and dropped it into her tea.

Then Mrs. Combs pushed her peas into her potatoes.

I leaned over and I said to Mama, I said, "Mama, go ahead and chew your ice."

And she said to me, she said, "Not tonight, Belva Jean. I'm playing Emily Vanderbilt."

I was beginning to wish I hadn't made such a big to-do over everything. Mama could have done anything she wanted and she still would have fit in. In fact, she was just about the most normal mother there.

What Granny Kept in Her Grips

Granny Stilts, she come up from Arkansas on the train — she's askeered of planes — and I tell you, you never saw such a load of suitcases (only Granny calls them grips). She had her a footlocker, a big old one, dark green, and three regular suitcases, all sizes, and a little square box with a handle like an overnight case, and a wardrobe bag so crammed full it wouldn't bend.

But that was only what come off the luggage rack. Here's what she was carrying herself — a big, round box with a handle that Mama said was for hats, two shopping bags filled with boxes, a knitting bag, a lunch box, and a big, navy blue pocketbook. We was fit to be tied, carrying all them grips to the car. Mama said to

21

Granny, "What did you think you was gonna do, Mom, stay for a year?"

"Delia, I got to have my things," was all she said.

When we got home we took all Granny's bags, boxes, and grips up to my room. I've got the front room in the attic. She opened up her foot-locker on the cedar chest and all them grips she opened up across the floor. You couldn't hardly walk across the room without tripping over one of them. So what I done for the two weeks she was there, I would make a running start out in the hall and dive onto the bed.

But I got to tell you about the presents she brought. She dug them out of her grips and shopping bags and we carried them all down-stairs. Most all the gifts was wrapped in white tissue paper with yellow, crinkly bows.

First of all, she had crocheted slippers for each of us — yellow for Mama, pink for me, blue for Buster, and purple for Daddy. Purple with tassles.

Daddy said, "Thanks, them are exactly what I need." He put them on and wore them around the house for the rest of the day, just to be polite. But I knew the minute she was gone,

Daddy would give them to Mama to sell at her next garage sale.

That ain't all she had for us. She'd been making wreaths out of pine cones, gathering them pine cones in the woods out back of her house, and she had a wreath for each of us, including Buster. She said we was to put them on our doors inside the house. She even brought three extra so we could decorate the closets and the bathroom. Mama put them all up. I tell you there wasn't a door in the house that didn't have a wreath on it. Only we didn't have a wreath for our side entrance (we've got the second and third floors of our house and the landlord lives on the first), so Granny made us one out of pine cones she found in our backyard. She said wreaths was a sign of welcome and we ought to have one on our entrance.

But I got to tell you what else Granny had. She brought us each a special present. Mama, she brought her a genuine Ozark cookbook made by the ladies of the Goshen County Hospital Ladies Auxiliary. It had in it things like Lightnin' Cake and Poppin' Blueberry Muffins. It also had things like how to butcher a hog in six easy steps and how to make hand soap in

23

your own backyard. Then, Daddy, she brought him a genuine Ozark thumb piano. (She called it a pie-ana.) It was half a gourd with a wooden top and some little bitty metal keys that you pluck. Daddy promised he would pick out a tune on it before she left. Buster, he's two, she brought him a little wooden dancing doll. You set it on a piece of wood and jiggle it and it dances. And me—well, me, she brought me some plastic shoes she said was called "jellies." I didn't much like them, but she said all the girls was wearing them down in Precious. That's the town in Arkansas where she lives.

"How do you like them?" Granny was grinning because she thought she'd brought me something real popular.

"They're nice," I said.

"Nice for rain," Granny said.

I put them in my closet, hoping she wouldn't ask me why I wasn't wearing them to school.

Then Granny come on upstairs and we unpacked the rest of her grips. In one, she had home cures. She lined them up across the windowsill and told me what they was for—pine needles in sorghum for cough, sumac tea for hay fever, rattlesnake weed for stomach, a poultice of red clay and vinegar for bruises (though she said she didn't have no bruises at the time, that the poultice was just in case), and sassafras tea for healthy blood. She said to me, "You should take you some of this sassafras tea, Belva Jean. It'll purify your blood."

Then she had another grip filled with white underwear that was like droopy long shorts and they was cotton knit.

"What are those?" I said.

"Belva Jean, them are snuggies," she said. "You should get you some. They'll keep you nice and warm. I wear them under my dresses."

"In May?"

"Yes, of course. There's still a chill out there."

Then she set out her hair curlers — long metal sticks with a clasp. They were like barrettes, only she would take and wrap her hair around each one and fasten, and she would have big spokes sticking out in every direction around her head.

In the little overnight case she had special potions for her complexion. Now, I got to admit Granny has a nice complexion, but to keep it that way she goes to a powerful lot of trouble.

She said to me, "Belva Jean, you're a young

lady now, old enough to start thinking about keeping nice skin. How about letting Granny treat you to a facial?"

Well, I was only at the tail end of sixth grade and didn't think I needed to worry much about my skin, but I brought in a chair and a towel and a basin of water, anyway. Might as well see what she done.

First thing she done was she painted on a red mask from a mayonnaise jar of something.

"What's that?" I said.

"Beet juice," she said. "I brewed this out of the tops."

"What's that supposed to do?"

"Brings out the bloom of youth."

"But I am a youth," I said.

"Yes, I know," she said, "but this will help you to *bloom*."

So we let that sit for a while. Then she took it off and put on some whitish cream from a French's mustard jar.

"What's this?" I said.

"Cream and honey."

"Well, what's *it* supposed to do?"

"This is to bring the boys around." Then she said to me, "Belva Jean, do you like the boys?"

"Sort of," I said.

"I 'spect you will. This will bring them around."

So she smeared this sticky, white cream on my face and told me how, when she was young, the boys would all follow her home, "by the dozen," she said, "and Mama — that's your *great*-grandma — used to have to shoo them off the front porch."

So we let that sit awhile. Then she said, "Belva Jean, I'll bet your mama never told you she sneaked out of the house one day to go roller skating with a boy from Camden City."

"No," I said. I didn't think my mama ever sneaked to go nowhere.

"Well, she did," Granny said. "Mama don't tell you these things, but Granny, she will. She's not askeered." Granny made it sound as if it was her duty. "She was gone with him a whole day and they even went over to Tantamount Creek and went wading."

"Yeah?" I said. "How did you know?"

"Granny's friend was that boy's mama, and I found out."

"What did you do?"

"Well, I couldn't say nothing because I wasn't

supposed to know. So I just hid her skates for a couple of weeks."

"And what did Mama do?"

"Well, she couldn't say nothing because she didn't want to bring up what she knew I knew."

"So she never said nothing about her skates?"

"Granny knows best." She started to undo the lid on another one of her potions, then said, "You ever done anything sneaky, Belva Jean? Come on, you can tell Granny. She won't tell."

I figured that anything I told Granny she would right away go tell Mama. But I told her something, anyway. "You know them Christmas presents you sent last year?"

"Yes," Granny said.

"Well, I sneaked into all of them before Christmas."

Granny started to giggle. "I used to sneak into presents, too," she said.

She took the white cream off; then she put on something that looked like tea, from an old Coke bottle.

"What's this for?" I said.

"This is to smooth out the wrinkles," she said. "'Course you don't have none yet, so for you it's prevention."

So we done the facial and washed and wiped my face clean. Then she dusted it with pure, white powder.

"What's that?" I said.

"Cornstarch," she said. "Like Snow White."

"Feels funny," I said. Then I looked in the mirror. My eyelashes was all caked up so I looked like one of them stars in a spook movie.

"It's what I've used since I was a girl," she said.

I thought we was all finished but Granny had one last piece of advice. "If you ever get chapped lips, Belva Jean," she said, "kiss the middle rail of a five-rail fence."

"But there's no five-rail fences around here," I said.

"That's right," she said. "Well, look for a three-railer. That'll do."

I really suspected that kissing a wooden railing could make your chapped lips worse — especially if it had splinters in it — but I never argued with Granny. I argued with my mama, but not with Granny.

One thing I knowed, though. If you stayed around with Granny when she was unpacking her grips, she would tell you what was in them and a whole lot more besides.

The Fourth of July Party

We was having breakfast one Saturday when we first moved in, and Mama was looking out the back window, down at the neighbors' yard, and she said, "Looks like they got a nice little boy next door."

"How old?" I said.

"Looks like your age."

I went over to the window to see what she meant by "nice little boy," and by the time I got to our door another boy had come out, just a little younger. They looked pretty much alike, wearing red sweaters and white tennis shoes. Their door opened up again and out come two girls, about seven and eight. We thought that was just about the end. Then the door opened

31

again and out come two more, both boys.

Then Mama said, "I wonder just how many kids those people have."

Well, the door kept opening up until there was ten kids out there, some of them twins, we guessed, all in sweaters, mostly red and navy blue, and all of them in sneakers. My guess was that they never wore out them sneakers. They just passed them along.

"Ten kids," Mama said. "How do they feed them all?"

Thing is, there was really twelve. The baby was in the crib and there was another one on the way.

They didn't have much trouble feeding them, though, because their grandpa, who lived with them, owned a vegetable market.

"It looks like you got a nice lot of playmates," Mama said.

"Only *one* my age," I said.

But I went over there later on that morning and I swung on their swings and climbed on their jungle gym. Then they come over to my yard and dug in my dirt. They went to the Catholic school. We was all good friends, especially me and Faron. He was the oldest of the Lavellas.

We just went back and forth from his yard to mine all summer.

Then come the Fourth of July. Firecrackers was going off all over the neighborhood, and Mama and I looked out the window. Grandpa Lavella was stringing little colored flags around the yard — you know, like they put up at a new gas station or a pizza parlor.

"I'm getting dressed and going down," I said.

"And you'll stay in *your* yard, Belva Jean," Mama said.

"Why?"

"When a family is a-having company, you do not go over and make a pest of yourself."

"I'm not a pest," I said, and I went downstairs.

None of the kids was up, but Grandpa Lavella, he was bringing chairs from a truck that was backed up into their driveway. It was from the Our Lady of the Holy Redeemer, Sacrificed. He was bringing the chairs and two other men was bringing the tables, long ones like they got at the bingo games.

All this time I was just walking back and forth along our hedge, trying to figure out a way to get to go. I couldn't ask Grandpa Lavella, even though he was nice, because he couldn't hear that good and he was playing them Italian opera records full blast. Then I saw Faron and his dad come out. I knew what I would do — ask Faron to ask his dad.

Problem is, Mama, she leaned down out of our second-floor window and called out, loud enough for Faron's daddy to hear, "Now, Belva Jean, you stay in your own yard. The Lavellas is having a party."

Shucks, I thought. I'll just have to have Faron ask his mother. Meanwhile, Faron and his brother and daddy, they was bringing in the food. You never saw such a picnic. They took a whole, long aluminum bathtub (I guess that's what it was) and stuffed it with watermelon and huge chunks of ice. Then there was about six round tubs filled with cans of pop, all kinds. And a big freezer box full of Eskimo pies and popsicles. Then they had a long barbecue pit they set up next to a little Arabian tent.

Mama yelled out again, "Now, Belva Jean, you stay in your yard."

Faron, he walked over to the fence, and he said, "I asked my mom if you could come, but she said it's only for relatives."

"Shucks," I said. "But I'm your best friend."

34

"I know," he said, and he went over and snuck me a can of pop. I got tired of standing there by the hedge, though, so I climbed up into our tree. I could see pretty good from up there.

Faron helped his daddy fill their fish pond up, and one of his little sisters put a statue of Mary over the waterfall.

Then the relatives started to come. You never saw so many relatives. There was another family, just like the Lavellas, with about eight kids, all of them in look-alike T-shirts. And they was all noisy, running around with special cap hammers and little flags Grandpa Lavella gave them. Then there was aunts and uncles, dozens of them.

Once in a while, someone would shoot some fireworks off—a pinwheel or a jumping jack— down their side yard.

Faron brought me over an Eskimo pie and I was just about to ask him to ask his mama again, but then my mama yelled out, "Now, Belva Jean, I've told you it's the *Lavellas'* party."

So Faron went back with his cousins and I climbed back up into the tree. Then I decided that being up in the tree wouldn't get me nowhere. None of the Lavellas could see me. So I climbed down and got me a ladder out of the

garage. I set it next to the hedge, climbed up, and sat on the top step.

Still didn't nobody notice me, except Mama. She yelled down, "Belva Jean, you come up here this minute."

So I went up.

And she said, "Belva Jean, you put that ladder away."

"Why?" I said. "I'm not bothering nobody."

"You're making a fool of yourself."

"I am not."

Mama was in a bad mood because Buster was sick with a cold.

Then Daddy got in on it. He said, "If she wants to make a fool of herself, then let her. There's worse things she could be doing." So while they was going back and forth on whether or not I should play the fool, I went and got the binoculars out of the kitchen, put them around my neck, and went downstairs.

Then I climbed up on my ladder and looked through them so's I could see what-all was going on in the far corners of the yard. The kids under the Arabian tent had a race-car track they'd set up. And they was all eating big pieces of watermelon. Faron's mom, she was handing out

37

little squares with white cheese and olives on top, and deviled eggs, it looked like.

Faron come over to the fence with a piece of watermelon he'd snuck me, and I said, "Go ask again." But I saw him go over, and his mama said no, so I climbed back up and just sat there hoping for some sort of miracle. I thought they might need somebody to keep score in the volleyball or to hold up the net or to take the place of an injured player.

Why didn't we never have parties like that, is what I wondered. The biggest party we ever had was Granny. Or sometimes men from Daddy's thermometer factory.

So I just sat up there, watching everything. Pretty soon Mr. Lavella asked who wanted to be in an egg toss. There was eight pairs that volunteered. They started out tossing them eggs real close, then got farther and farther apart. Everybody was yelling and screaming. One of Faron's aunts got an egg busted on her skirt. Another egg landed in the fish pond. Then it was down to a couple of Faron's cousins and his grandpa and uncle. Faron's cousins won.

Then two of the uncles started tossing a Frisbee. They tossed it back and forth by the fish pond; then they spread out and were sailing that thing over the food, over everybody's head. One of them couldn't throw too straight. He almost hit Faron's mama. Then he throwed it too hard, and it sailed right over the hedge and up my way. I let go of my binoculars, stood up on the ladder, and caught it in one hand. I just about fell over — the ladder teetered — I dropped my piece of watermelon, but I got my balance and come down to the hedge to give them the Frisbee.

That's when Grandpa Lavella said, "Come on over, you come to the party, too."

He was a real nice man, could tell good stories and blow cigar smoke out his ears.

Faron said, "I knew you'd get to come, sooner or later."

And did we have a time. I played volleyball, ran a three-legged race with Faron, sat up on the fish pond and hammered caps, then jumped on a trampoline Grandpa Lavella brought in for the kids. And here's what I ate (besides what Faron give me before) — two ice cream bars, one hot dog, two hamburgers, two pieces of chicken, some potato salad, three brownies, six cans of pop, and three apples.

Mama looked down from the window and waved for me to come home, but Faron yelled up, "She's *invited!*"

39

Me and Buster

One day, when I was looking after Buster, and we was both sitting there eating zwieback toast and building a tower out of milk-carton blocks, we heard a lot of sirens. It wasn't just one siren from one truck, but lots of them. I looked out the window and counted three fire trucks pass down our street and turn the corner.

Buster, even he was pointing to the window, wondering what was going on. Well, I knowed Mama wanted me to stay inside with Buster till she got back from town, but here was something important going on, something that Buster should know about. So I cleaned Buster's face off real good, then went and got Buster's stroller and carried the both of them downstairs. I put

Buster in, then rolled him down the sidewalk. I said, "Buster, you're going to see a fire."

"Fi?" Buster said. He could talk a little, sometimes in sentences. "Buster dink harter" was one. It meant, "I want a drink of water." I was the first one to figure that out.

"Yes, and I want you to pay attention to everything I tell you." I talk to Buster a lot. When he was born, I read him stories and showed him cartoon pictures. Mama said reading to an infant was a waste of time, but I think Buster understood some of what I read. He always laughed at the jokes.

"Keep your hands in your lap," I said, and I showed him where his lap was, "and listen to everything I tell you."

Me and Buster, we followed them trucks down the street to where they went around the corner. And I leaned over and said to Buster, "Them's fire trucks, Buster. They got men on them and they're gonna fight the fire."

"Fi?" Buster said. Then he kicked and pointed.

"Fire," I said. I need to help him with his *r*'s.

Other people was coming out of their houses, looking down the street, and one lady yelled, "I think it's the A & P."

I said to Buster, "This is a *big* fire, Buster."

"Big fi," Buster said, and he made a sound like a siren.

Pretty soon there was a bunch of people behind and in front of us, all of us crossing the street in the middle of the block. One woman come out of her house with a towel wrapped around her bathing suit.

Once we got up to Main Street, it was like the whole town was out. Men was coming out of the barber shop wearing them white smocks. Everybody was walking real fast.

I leaned over and I said to Buster, "This may look like a circus, Buster, but it ain't. Some people get real excited, but we got to stay calm."

"Com?" Buster said.

"Yes," I said. "Calm."

We heard more sirens and soon's we got around the corner of the Futurama Furniture Store, we seen the smoke. Black and thick, like thunderclouds.

"That," I said, "there. That's smoke."

"Moke?" Buster said.

"Smoke," I said. I need to help him with his *s*'s.

The police was sending the cars down Galen Avenue so they could block off the street in front of the A & P.

I said to Buster, "They're blocking the traffic, Buster, so's all the firemen can get through." And I pointed out the fire trucks.

I heard one woman say to another, "Well, I hope they got everybody out."

"Yes, they did," another woman said. "There was an electrical problem in the freezer — something sparked and exploded, then everybody ran."

I leaned down and I said to Buster, "Don't never touch nothing electrical if your hands is wet."

"Had wet?" he said.

"Yes," I said. "Hands."

Me and Buster, we got up on the lawn in front of the war plaque. We had us a good view. There was six fire trucks, and at least as many hoses, so thick, a whole bunch of firemen had to hold them. They took axes and broke the plate-glass windows.

"They're doing that, Buster, so's they can get the water in." We could hear lots of explosions in the store, too. "Them's canned goods popping," I said to Buster.

"Bopping?" Buster said.

"Popping." I need to help him with his *p*'s.

We seen a lot of people coming out of the deli with heros and drinks.

"See, Buster, some people like to have refreshments when they watch a fire. But me and you, we already had some zwieback."

The firemen would shoot a stream of water and everyone would cheer. And the smoke kept getting blacker.

"You see, Buster," I said. "That black smoke is poison. You don't never want to breathe poison."

"Boisin?" Buster said.

"That's right," I said, "and if you're in your room and you smell smoke, don't never open the door. Just feel it first."

Buster kicked and pointed.

The roof caved in and they aimed more water over the top. Smoke poured out; then the flames died down.

"You see, Buster, it's almost over."

"Moke, fi!" Buster said.

"Yes, Buster, you're a smart boy."

We got back before Mama got home. I took Buster out of the stroller and carried it and Buster upstairs. Then me and him went back to building a tower and eating zwieback. I didn't tell nobody where we went that day. Daddy would say what I done was dangerous, and Mama would say explaining about fires was a waste of time on Buster. But I think Buster understands more than they think he does.

Uncle Abraham's Cabin

It never fails. Along about August, Daddy's sister, Aunt Loretta, calls up Mama and says she thinks it's time.

And Mama, I'll hear her on the phone saying, "Yes, it is. Yes, it is time. Time it is." And she'll call into Daddy, "Darwin, Loretta says it's time."

And Daddy, he'll say, "Well, if it's time, then it's time."

And I'll be thinking, oh, no, time, not again, it's time. Time to visit Uncle Abraham's cabin. We got to spend a whole day down there. That's Daddy's uncle, down in Personville, Kentucky. It's the same thing, every year, and I can tell you that the more *samer* it gets, the more Mama and Daddy seem to like it.

Aunt Loretta, she'll show up about nine Saturday morning with Uncle Harvey and Cousin Ruthie—though Ruthie seems more like an aunt, her being the same age as my mama. Cousin Odell, too. He's the same age as Daddy. He'll come with his wife, Clarice, and their baby daughter, Suzette. She's two. Buster's playmate. What a pair.

I'd like to get out of going, but Mama says if I stay home I got to forfeit playing outside for two weeks. She says Uncle Abraham is my oldest living relative and we got to go down and pay him respect. So I put on my best jeans and I get into the truck. Mama, she holds Buster, Daddy drives, and I'm a-sitting there in the middle. Aunt Loretta and Uncle Harvey follow us, then comes Ruthie in her MG, then Odell, Clarice, and Suzette. It's a four-car motorcade with Daddy's truck in the lead.

We drive through DeSailles, then onto Columbia Parkway, then over the Ohio River on Interstate 75. Daddy, he'll look through his rearview mirror every so often to make sure everyone's behind him. Once Odell got stuck at a light, so Daddy drove real slow till he had time to catch up.

We go down I-75 till we get to Georgetown, then we turn off on Kentucky 460, go a ways till we get to a town called Arthur, then on to Personville, which has one general store, a post office, a restaurant called the Melody Inn, and a showroom for tractors. Then we make some more turns and the road gets narrower and narrower until it's just about a mix of dirt and blacktop, and we're all bouncing along, Mama and Daddy having the same conversation they had last year and the year before that, and the next year it'll be even samer.

Daddy, he'll say, "Uncle Abraham, he used to box."

And Mama, she'll say, "Welterweight champion of Delphi County, wasn't he, Darwin?"

"Defended his title three times. Quite a man."

"Yes."

Then Daddy, he'll say, "Never come to our house but that he'd bring us kids something."

"Bag of licorice, wasn't it?" Mama will say.

"Or some firecrackers. One time he brought me a paint set."

"Quite an artist, wasn't he?" Mama will say.

"Why, he could paint a snowcapped mountain to look better than the real thing."

Sometimes they'll forget something, so I'll help them out. "And he used to fish in the Green River, didn't he, Daddy?"

"Quite a fisherman," Daddy, he'll say. "He'd bring in them big ones."

So we'll keep this up until we get to Uncle Abraham's cabin. It's a-way up in the woods, a white cabin with a tin roof and an old garage off to one side. We'll pull off the road and park diagonal, all of us, get out and stretch and unload. And the picnic we bring is the same this year as the year before and the year before that. Mama, she brings the baked beans and the potato salad, Aunt Loretta, she brings the sandwiches, Clarice and Odell, they bring the chips and dip, and Ruthie, she brings the pop. We carry it all around to the back since the front door's been nailed shut (for thirty years, Daddy says), and then Aunt Loretta, she'll knock on the door and holler for Uncle Abraham.

Out back I always look for Uncle Abraham's yellow cat, Sabbatical. She's usually sitting up in the persimmon tree.

Finally Uncle Abraham hollers that the door's unlocked. So we go in and there sits Uncle Abraham in his usual spot, dead center in the middle of the kitchen on his wooden chair, with his hat on. He don't have no TV, so he sort of faces the radio. His bed is in there, against the wall. That room, the kitchen, is the only part of the cabin he uses. (Of course there's the bathroom, added onto the kitchen about the same time the front door was nailed shut, Daddy says.)

"Well, how're you doing?" Daddy'll say first.

"All right, okay," Uncle Abraham'll say.

"Well, you're looking good," Uncle Harvey, he'll say.

"Thanks," Uncle Abraham will say. And he'll pull his hat down a little further and button up his shirt.

"Well," Clarice will say, looking around, "your cabin looks real nice." And we all sort of look around. There's a sign up on the wall that says "We too soon old and too late smart," and one of Uncle Abraham's old paintings—a baby deer standing in a pool of green water. Then there's a wall full of canned soups, mostly minestrone.

"Is Lula still buying your groceries?" Mama will ask. Lula's the lady down the road who does the shopping for Uncle Abraham.

"Yep," Uncle Abraham will say.

"Well, ain't that nice," Mama will say.

51

They always say the same things to Uncle Abraham, then get right into the food, and the whole thing turns into a big picnic. Mama and Aunt Loretta set it all out on the kitchen table. Ruthie hands out the paper plates; then everyone helps himself.

Aunt Loretta, she makes Uncle Abraham a plate and they have the same conversation they had last year.

"I see you got your wood stove cleaned up and ready to go," Loretta'll say.

"Yep, it's a good stove," Uncle Abraham'll say.

"Gonna be a hard winter, I can feel it," Odell, he'll say.

"You be sure and let us know if you need anything," Daddy, he'll say.

"This cabin's built real solid," Ruthie, she'll say.

"Yep," Uncle Abraham'll say. "It don't leak rain, and cold air don't come in."

Me, Mama, Loretta, Ruthie, and Clarice, we're a-sitting on the bed (lined up like we was guèsts on a talk show) and all the men, they're a-sitting on wire milk cartons. Buster and Suzette, they're all over the floor.

We keep talking until everybody's full of

potato chips, pop, and sandwiches. Then Mama and Aunt Loretta, they put the food back into the boxes, and Odell, he'll say, "Well, Uncle Abraham, how about a ride?"

"Oh, I don't know," Uncle Abraham, he'll say, same as he said last year.

"Ah, come on, Uncle Abraham, it'll do you good," Daddy, he'll say.

Finally Uncle Harvey, Cousin Odell, and Daddy will get him out to Cousin Odell's car, and Daddy, he'll take Suzette and Buster "to keep them out of your hair," he'll say to Mama, then Aunt Loretta will say, same as she said last year, "All right, gals, let's go to it."

As soon as the men drive off, all of us run out to the cars and bring in the cleaning equipment. Mama, she brings the scrub brush, ammonia, dust cloths and Windex. Aunt Loretta, she brings the vacuum, dust mop and brooms. Ruthie, she brings clean sheets, pillowcase, and lemon wax, and Clarice, she brings the Comet cleanser, Oven-Off, paper towels, and sponges.

We go real fast because we ain't got that much time. Me, I do the windows, Mama does the bathroom, Aunt Loretta, she takes the floors, Ruthie changes the sheets and polishes the bookcase, and Clarice, she tackles the sink and the stove.

And all this time, we'll be saying the same things we said last year.

Aunt Loretta, she'll say, "I swear I never seen so many dust balls. Uncle Abraham would die of dust if it wasn't for us a-coming up each year."

Mama, she'll say, "I swear, Uncle Abraham

would die of germs if it wasn't for me a-cleaning up his bathroom."

Ruthie, she'll say, "Same sheets he had last year, I swear. It's time he was sleeping on new ones."

Clarice, she'll say, "I never seen so much grease on one sink in my life, I swear."

And me, I'm not about to be outdone. I'll say, "These windows, I swear. It's a wonder Uncle Abraham can tell if it's day or night."

So we're going as fast as we can, "cleaning up on the sly," Aunt Loretta calls it, and we'll clean up that whole cabin, until it's a-shining like a penny. Then we'll hurry up take everything back out to the car and be lined up sitting on the bed when Uncle Abraham and the men come back, "just as if we've been sitting here the whole time," says Aunt Loretta, feeling real proud of everything.

Thing is, no way can Uncle Abraham help but smell the stink of the ammonia, Comet cleanser, and lemon wax when he comes in. Only he never says nothing. Just acts like as if it's normal. Same this year as last year. I think he don't mind it at all, getting his cabin cleaned.

And there'll be sly winks going back and forth

between the men and women, and Mama, she'll say, "Uncle Abraham, it's about time we was leaving you. It's been a good visit."

She'll give him a kiss and we'll all line up and give him one — I swear, it gets scratchier each year — then we'll all head on back to DeSailles.

Standard English

Maybe I'm only eleven, but people are always asking me what I want to be when I grow up. So I say either I want to be a TV-talk-show host, or discover a prevention for warts. Mama says, whatever I do, I should be a lady.

One day she was reading the paper and she come across this ad from Loden's Department Store that they was giving a free Modeling and Self-Improvement course on Saturdays down at their store. So Mama said to me, she said, "Belva Jean, I think we should sign you up."

And I said, "Mama, this ain't gonna help me with my life goals." (Life goals, I'd heard that on TV.)

"Belva Jean," she said, "are you aware that

Delilah Davis was once a model?"

Delilah Davis is our local TV-talk-show host. "She was?"

"She was a Caumsett Model right here in town."

"That don't mean nothing."

"Well, think of it this way, Belva Jean. You've got the opportunity to self-improve yourself. Says here they discuss proper skin care for girls and teens, modeling techniques for poise and self-assurance, and how to develop yourself for your future career."

"Future career?" I said. "I'm only eleven."

"Three sessions," Mama said. "It can't hurt. Besides, it's *free*." Anything that was free got Mama excited. "Besides, Daddy can take you downtown in the truck and you can spend the rest of the day fooling around downtown, then take the bus home. Wouldn't that be nice?"

You could tell she was real anxious for me to go, and to tell the truth, I was curious what it would be like. Besides, I thought, when I grow up, maybe I could be a model during the daytime and host a TV talk show at night. Weekends I could look for a prevention for warts.

So I said okay, but let me go with JaneEllen Hazard. So Mama called her mama and they called up Loden's and we was signed up. It's a good thing they done it right away because we read in the paper they was swamped. Some girls would have to wait a year to get in.

Anyway, Daddy took us down on Saturday. It was from ten to twelve in a meeting room behind the ladies' third-floor lounge. I knew where the lounge was but I didn't know there was a meeting room behind it. Me and JaneEllen was among the first. We took a seat near the back and watched the other girls come in. They was from other schools all over town and come in in little groups.

The room filled up pretty quick and it felt sort of like a school class. We even had the kind of seats that have an arm that you can write on. Then in come this woman in a navy blue suit and short blond hair with round, red earrings. She said, "Good morning, ladies." And she stood behind a lectern. "My name is Niki Simms," she said. She wrote her name up on a blackboard and said we could call her Niki.

"I'll tell you our plans for the three weeks," she said. "We'll talk about proper face and body care this first week, and I'll want to talk to each of you about your face shape and your most becoming hairdo, and I'll want to find out what your goals are."

"Now, why would *she* want to know?" I said to JaneEllen.

"Beats me," JaneEllen said.

"The second week," Niki continued, "we'll talk about diet and exercise, and the third week we'll practice runway modeling. Then for graduation, we'll have a fashion show on Friday evening of the twenty-third, and you'll model your favorite outfit for your parents."

Everyone seemed happy that we would be in a real fashion show.

"I thought they was just going to have us pretend," JaneEllen said.

One girl wanted to know if she could wear her mother's fur stole.

"We'll discuss clothes at our last session," Niki said. Then she got right into our lesson, Face and Body Care. She started out by telling us how to wash our faces. "Never use soap," she said.

I looked at JaneEllen and JaneEllen looked at me. "And never take a bath, neither," I whispered.

61

But Niki said, "Use cleansing cream instead." She showed us some different kinds of cleansing cream — she had them all lined up on a cart. Then she had one girl come up and sit on a stool while she done her face, rubbing that cleansing cream in in a "circular motion," as Niki said. (Granny would have liked this session, but I think she would have argued for beet juice.)

Niki said you should do that in the morning and at night and that if you didn't, you could get ugly blemishes and blackheads, "which are so unbecoming," she said.

Niki told us about a lot of things that was unbecoming. Here's what I remember best:

> *wearing blue eyeshadow*
> *biting your nails*
> *crossing your legs at the knees instead*
>   *of the ankles*
> *popping gum*
> *talking to boys when your hair is not perfect*

Niki sort of worked all that in while she done the girl's face and makeup.

Then she done a short talk on nutrition,

mostly what I'd already learned in school.

One girl wanted to know if eating carrots would curl your hair.

Niki said, "Not to my knowledge, but they are a good source of vitamin A."

Then Niki asked us all to line up so that we could tell her what our ambitions were, and she could study the shape of our face and tell us what hairstyle was most becoming.

I heard her tell the girl before me she had a heart-shaped face and should fluff her hair out on the sides, "to add a little more fullness to your jaw," she said.

Then my turn came. She looked at me real close for a while, sort of from eyes to chin and chin to eyes and she said, "Your face is a 'diamond,' so you need fullness at the top and at the bottom. Curls would be nice. Now tell Niki what you would like to be."

"I ain't quite sure yet," I said, "but I think I want to be a scientist and a TV-talk-show host."

She didn't say nothing for a few seconds and I thought she was maybe going to ask me what kind of talk show I wanted to do. But then she whispered, "Your English. You'll have to work on your English."

I didn't know what she meant at first, and even though she whispered this, I was afraid everybody could hear. I didn't say nothing else. I was afraid the next thing I said, even if it was one word, would be wrong. So I waited for JaneEllen Hazard.

JaneEllen's face was "the inverted triangle," so she needed fullness at the top and to brush hair over her jaw. JaneEllen said she wanted to be a nurse, and Niki told her she looked like a nice, kind, sweet person.

Me and JaneEllen had lunch at Nanette's, in the arcade, but I still couldn't get over what Niki had said. I didn't even know if I wanted to go back. I said to JaneEllen, "I talk the way my mama talks and my daddy talks, and my aunt Loretta and my granny Stilts."

"She means you say *ain't*," JaneEllen said. "Just quit saying 'ain't' and 'we was' and 'he come.' Just talk the way we write at school, you know, when we're having them, I mean those, composition tests."

Mama was waiting for me in the kitchen to hear how I done at the Modeling and Self-Improvement class. "Well, how was it?" she said.

You could tell she was real anxious for me to like it, but I said it was dumb. I told Mama what Niki the model said, and Mama said, "Just who does she think she is, telling you your English is funny. You talk the way you want to."

Then she went over to the sink and peeled some potatoes. But I knew what Niki had said had gotten to her because she come back to me and said, "A person can be a good person and smart no matter what they talk like. Look at your great-granddaddy Stilts. He was a state representative and he talked just like the rest of us."

"But he was from the country," I said. "Besides, he didn't have to go on TV."

"TV ain't important," she said. And she went back to the sink. But I guess she realized what she'd said, me wanting to be a talk-show host and all. Because she come back to me a few minutes later, and she said, "We talk like country people, Belva Jean. Maybe you should learn how to talk right."

"My teacher at school says I do talk right," I said. "It's just different. She said it's a dialect. And what she teaches at school is Standard English."

"Well, then let's speak Standard English sometimes," said Mama. "I want to learn, too."

We didn't know quite how to go about it, but we thought maybe if we got us some books, we could learn from them. So we went to the library, but we didn't end up with no books. We decided we needed to *hear* Standard English, so we looked through the records. Mama went over to the Shakespeare section first and started to grab some albums. "Might as well start with the best," she said.

"But people don't talk that way now," I said. "Get something that's modern."

Then we looked through a section called "Readings" and found things like "Jennifer Miles Reads *A Child's Garden of Verses*" and "Leonard Bascomb Reads 'The Gettysburg Address.'"

Then Mama said, "How about this?" and she pulled down an album called "Speak English." "Look at what it says here," she said. "'Six weeks from today, speak this language fluently with a perfect American accent!'"

"We *are* American," I said.

"*Too* American," Mama said. "We got a country accent."

"I still don't know how this is going to help when it's made for Italians," I told Mama.

"Don't matter who it's for," Mama said. "All we'll listen for is the English."

So we took it home, and what do you know, the whole thing is in English. They have a little book so Italians can read in their own language what the English means. We played a little bit of the first record, but all they was doing was reciting American names and going through the numbers and colors. But the other records, now them was what we needed. They had little speeches in them for doing different things like taking your clothes to the dry cleaners, or buying aspirin at the drugstore, or asking how to get to the post office. Here's one on taking a dress back:

Excuse me, ma'am. This dress is too large.
Oh, would you like to exchange it?
Yes, I would. Do you have a size ten?
Yes, we do. Here it is.
Thank you very much.
You're welcome.

I said to Mama, "Don't you think that Italian woman should have tried on the size ten first?"

"Yes," Mama said, "but she probably didn't know the words to ask."

So even though some of them speeches could

have made more sense, me and Mama practiced them whenever we was in the mood.

And sometimes we would sort of speak that way, making up our own dialogue. Mama would say something like, "Excuse me, Belva Jean. Is that your shoe sitting there in the middle of the floor?"

"Yes, I believe it is, Mama. Why do you ask?"

"I would like you to take it upstairs, Belva Jean."

"All right, Mama."

"Thank you very much."

"You're welcome."

We was doing a lot of them routines at the dinner table every night. Just about drove Daddy up the wall.

We got so, too, we would listen real close to the TV set, try to talk exactly like the newscasters or whoever was on. I paid special attention to Delilah Davis. She said, "Howdy," at the beginning of her show, but that was the only country word she used.

The tough part was using this English at school. Some of the girls thought I was being uppity.

"We *were* going?" Dixie Lee imitated me saying one day. And Eva Jones said, "I *haven't* the time? My, my!" So I quit talking that way to people I made feel uncomfortable. JaneEllen Hazard, though, she knew what I was doing. And sometimes she would join in. "Belva Jean, I haven't a thing to wear Saturday and I am wondering what I shall do," she would say.

Sometimes I felt like I knew two languages.

"Niki might have done you a service," Mama said.

That week, when Mama and me was practicing our Standard English, I kept trying to think of things I would say to Niki in perfect grammar:

> Exercise isn't difficult if one is in shape.
> Is exercise difficult if one is in shape?
> No, exercise is good for one who is in shape.

So when we went in and we was doing them exercises, and she took us aside to tell us if we needed to lose or gain weight, I said, "These exercises aren't difficult if one does them often enough," and I looked at her real close to see if she noticed.

But she just said, "No, they're not."

Then I said, "I'm not fat and I'm not thin."

She said, "No, you're just right, and you're very lucky."

But she didn't say nothing about my English. I think Standard English is something that if you use it, nobody pays no attention. But if you don't use it, if I'd said, "I ain't fat and I ain't thin," she would have guessed all kinds of things about me. I mean she would have thought I was from

the country. And that I was poor. And maybe that I was stupid. But none of them is true.

Our third session she taught us how to model. We done things like walking around the room with a book on our head. Niki said this was very old-fashioned, but it developed our poise.

We spent most of our time learning how to pivot. You put one foot in front of the other

and sort of lift your heels and turn around on your toes. So we done that and she taught us our modeling routine. It was on a runway with stairs at both ends. You would walk up the stairs all the way to the middle, pivot, walk to the beginning, pivot, walk to the end, pivot, walk to the middle, pivot, and walk down.

Then Niki wanted to talk to each of us and tell us what our best colors was. She gave us each a chart, and we was studying it, but she knew at a glance which colors we looked best in.

"Let's see," she said to me. "You have light brown hair with gold highlights. Blue is your best color, but you would also look very nice in red."

"I haven't tried much blue," I said, "but I wore red many times last summer, and I found it very becoming."

"Of course," Niki said.

When we had the modeling show over at Loden's, Niki introduced each girl and told what school she went to and what she wanted to be. Then she gave each girl, when she come off the runway, a little diploma that said she was a graduate of the Loden Modeling and Self-Improvement class.

Mama went up to Niki when it was over, and she said, "My, you certainly have done wonders with these girls." Then she said to me, loud enough so that everyone could hear, "Belva Jean, you were really quite lovely, and you did your pivots with exquisite poise."

But I wanted to say one more thing to Niki. While everyone was walking off and Niki was putting the extra diplomas back in the box, I said, "Do you think I should be a model, a scientist, or a TV-talk-show host?"

She looked at me real close and said, "I think you could be anything you wanted to be."

So I knowed she could tell the difference. But I knowed it would take a long time to learn Standard English. You got to practice it the way you do a foreign language. But I intend to keep on working on it. My teacher at school says Demosthenes had a speech defect, so he practiced talking with pebbles in his mouth. If he learned to talk perfect with pebbles in his mouth, I can learn Standard English.

Afterword

Now, I could have told you these stories in Standard English, but I'm not on TV, and this ain't a formal occasion. This was just me rambling on about times I've had and people I've knowed, and things we've did together. So I hope, even if you're not from where I'm from, that you've liked my country speech. Anyway, I like talking this way with friends. And I hope you enjoyed listening.